THE FLYING COW

NEW YORK / HENRY Z. WALCK, INCORPORATED / 1963

THE FLYING COW

BY RUTH PHILPOTT COLLINS

PICTURES BY EZRA JACK KEATS

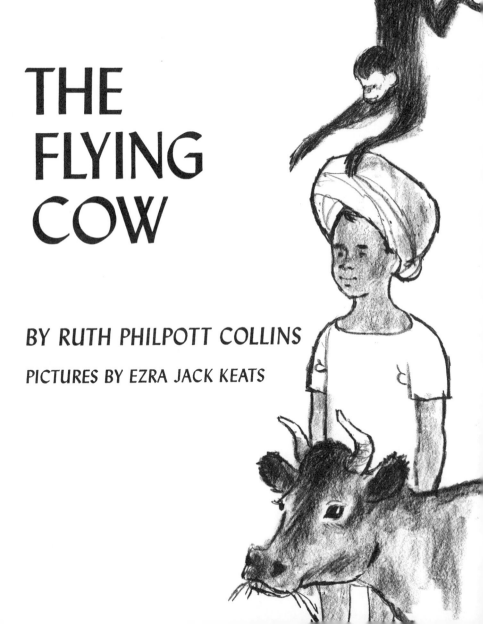

To my granddaughter

KATHLEEN MENZIES COUPER

Contents

1 The Juggler

"Rama! Rama! Rama!" The cry rose high over the court-yard wall.

It was barely dawn, but the little South India village was already wide awake. Rama, the weaver's son, was up in his old oxcart, singing at the top of his voice as usual, starting out on his day's journey. He stopped with an angry, "Look at that! Dumbir has let his buffaloes wander again." He frowned at the trail of the big clumsy hoofs through his grandmother's fine mustard patch.

Now he could hear her frantic call, "Rama! That monkey of yours is loose again. And chasing the villagers from the well. And the Rajah is out there. And . . ."

But Rama was already racing toward the well.

There was always a crowd around the Mango Tree Well at this hour of the morning since it lay on the way out to the paddy fields and the teakwood forest. Women in bright saris, waterpots piled high on head, gossiped with merchants on their heavily laden little donkeys. The creak of the old water wheel was quite lost in the *clap-clap* of the work-elephants' wooden bells, the hollow clatter of the herdboys' bamboo sticks on the bony rumps of their buffaloes, the shrill voices of small boys hurrying out to scare off the rice birds with tin cans and drums.

This morning though—and it was the first time Rama in all his fourteen years had ever seen such a sight—there was one of the royal elephants with red velvet robe and silver bells; and, riding in the howdah on top, the young Rajah himself, just newly returned home. With him was his pretty little daughter, Kamala, laughing and gay, with enormous dark eyes, marigolds braided in her long pigtails, bangles and jewels glittering in the first rays of the sun.

They were all laughing at the little gray monkey who, perched on a branch just out of reach, was trying to don a huge yellow turban while a furious old man stood threatening with a heavy stick below.

"Drop it, Moti! Drop it!" Rama shouted, running across and holding out his hands. But Moti, grinning, and jibbering, edged back along the branch till she was straight over the well then—*plop!*—down went the turban.

Everyone laughed but the juggler, for so the big reed basket in the road beside the angry old man showed him to be. He began to wail, lifting his hands toward the people in the howdah. "Alas, alas, my fine new turban!"

"Your fine new turban," a woman called out scornfully. "The monkey knew your dirty old rag needed a wash, juggler."

All laughed again but the juggler and the young Rajah in the howdah. He leaned out and said sternly, "Is that monkey yours, boy?"

"Yes, it's Rama's. And she's always up to mischief. Only yesterday she grabbed my stick and . . ." Dumbir, the herdboy, always ready to talk, was about to start off with another of his tales, but the villagers drowned him out.

"Nonsense. The monkey is just playing. The children love her," one cried.

You call it play when she pelts us with green mangoes . . ."

". . . and when she tears my sari to ribbons . . ."

". . . why, the monkey wouldn't hurt a fly. Remember how she used to roll around with that cheetah—all the tricks they were up to . . ."

Tricks. The old juggler forgot to wail and turned to look at Rama.

"Cheetah? Have you got a cheetah, boy?" the Rajah cried out eagerly.

"Oho," an old woman mumbled, "you see our young Rajah has the blood of his fathers after all. He talks now of cheetahs instead of goats. Soon he'll forget all this nonsense he learned across the seas, and we'll be having our festivals and elephant hunts as we used to. A good thing too. Who wants a herdboy for a rajah?"

But Rama was stammering out, "No, no, your Excellency, I have no cheetah now. He was just a baby one I found out in the long grass on the plain. He ran back to the jungle when he grew big."

"The weaver's boy is always dragging home wild things for his poor mother to feed," the old woman said.

"The weaver's son is a good boy," another put in.

"Ah," the Rajah looked across at the tumble-down mud wall behind, "so your father is the weaver?"

"The weaver was drowned in the big flood the year his son was born," a man explained.

"Along with his cow," the woman added, "and left only the ox and cart."

"And the weaving looms," the old woman reminded.

"What good are weaving looms in our village when the merchant here will buy only the cheap cloth from the factories in Madras?" the man asked bitterly.

"His mother will get ten rupees for the cloth she is weaving right now for the baker's wife," the old woman said enviously.

At this moment, though, Rama, who had been peering down into the well, fished out the turban and turned, beaming. "Here it is, here is your turban, juggler." He ran across and thrust it into the bony brown hand.

"Yes, but . . ." the juggler flapped the dripping cloth out, and his wails rose high again ". . . just look at it. All torn!"

"Turn it into a new one, juggler," one of the urchins cried out saucily.

At this point, however, there was a loud outcry from the howdah as the monkey, who had been hiding during all the talk, suddenly appeared out at the end of the branch and dropped down into the lap of the Rajah's daughter.

"Out, out, monkey, out!" the Rajah cried, but Moti had already twined her arms about Kamala, her tiny fingers pulling at her earring. "Call your monkey down, boy."

But Kamala's arms had tightened too about the monkey, and she begged, "No, no, let me keep her. I want her. I want her, *please*. . . ."

The Rajah hesitated. He looked down, saw Rama's

face, and said, "No, Kamala. The boy doesn't want to sell his pet. Come!" He reached for Moti, patted her head, and handed her down to Rama. "Keep this naughty little scamp of yours tied up, boy," he said kindly. He tossed a coin out to the juggler, glanced at his wrist watch, and called to the mahout, "Come, we must hurry! That cow will be flying in before we get there."

The elephant padded on swiftly. Kamala leaned out, pigtails flying in the wind, calling "Salaam, Moti, sala-am!" Rama stood holding his pet close.

But now there was a strange silence around the well. The juggler made no move to pick up the coin. He stood, wet turban in hand, his eyes blazing with hatred. And suddenly he shouted, "Did you hear what he said, villagers? A cow! One of those foreign cows flying down here to your village!"

"A flying cow?" the old woman said fearfully.

"Yes," Dumbir, the herdboy, broke in. "The Rajah told us all about it last night under the banyan tree. A great gold monster with long flowing tail and wings, spitting out fire and with a voice like thunder and enough milk in her udder for the whole village...."

"A cow with wings?" The old woman shook her head. "We have many strange gods on our temple walls, horses with wings and men with elephants' heads, and monkeys with men's heads—but a cow with wings? Oh, no, it sounds strange to me."

"Not any stranger than the other things that have been happening around here since the Rajah came home," a man cried out angrily. "For hundreds of years we have been living in this village as the Creator made it for us. Now see what has happened just since the last rains! One of those terrible motorcars tearing through our lanes. A great conker road for it across the plain, to get it to the railway station in an hour—a journey that takes a full day by oxcart. And..."

16

But now everyone joined in, a babel of voices either praising or blaming the young Rajah.

"He's turned the Rani's palace, which has been standing closed for years, into a fine school for our sons.... Yes, where Brahmins sit with outcastes. Bah!.... He's sold the elephants for his motorcar.... Yes, but you saw he was riding an elephant today across the muddy paddy fields.... He's taken down the palace gates so that all the villagers may enjoy the Rani's rose garden.... You mean turn it into pasture for this flying cow.... Yes, while our own sacred ones starve in the lanes.... And they say the students don't even learn letters—they learn how to milk a cow and grow grass...."

There was a general laugh at this for of course everyone knew how to milk a cow and grow grass. The old juggler, though, said nothing. He wound his wet turban on his head, took up his basket, and slipped unnoticed on out to the plain.

Rama's grandmother called out crossly from the courtyard gate, "Rama, I wanted those indigo leaves while the dew was still on them." And he, still clutching Moti close, hurried back to his oxcart.

II   The Juggler's Curse

"Come on, Moti, we can't carry any more." Rama
mopped his face with the end of his turban and climbed
into the cart, lanky brown legs dangling out close to
the bullock's tail. The monkey, arms already full, ripped
up another handful of grass and came sprinting back up
beside him, grinning happily.

It had been a long hard day out on the plain. The
spot where Rama usually found the wild indigo for
his mother's dye vat had been bare, and he had had to
wander on through the maze of cactus and anthills till
he found more. It had taken many scraggy plants to fill
the cart. He had ended up close to the jungle.

Usually he dawdled there, singing loudly, hoping for
an answering bark or a glimpse of the sleek gold-black-
dappled cheetah. Today he was silent. He let the old ox

graze just while he washed out his loincloth and turban in the little creek and then, with a loud *h-r-e-e-e*, hurried him on toward home. He did not sing. He kept an anxious eye on the sky half expecting at any moment to see a giant golden monster swooping down toward him. He jumped in alarm when Moti suddenly dropped her bit of sugar cane and sprang up into the bamboo rafters overhead for safety.

"What is it, little one?" Rama glanced up at the sky again, then around at the dusty cactus. All he could see were some green parrots coming noisily out of the bushes, a cloud of pink egrets rising from some reeds beyond. He poked back among the indigo leaves. Then, as the ox stopped and turned his long face inquiringly, Rama heard the thin, weird notes of a reed flute coming from somewhere nearby.

He made his way back in among the cactus and after a few steps came on the old juggler.

He was sitting, in dirty yellow robe and turban, cross-legged, in a small clearing, his big basket open on the ground beside him. His eyes were closed and his bony brown fingers, scarcely moving on the reed, were playing the same plaintive high note over and over again.

Rama edged in closer and peered into the basket. "But where is the cobra, snake charmer?" he cried.

The juggler dropped the flute, slammed on the lid

of his basket, and started up in a rage. "How dare you come spying on me, boy?" he shouted.

Rama backed away. "I'm not spying. I was just driving by with my load of indigo...."

"Ah," the old man was scrambling to his feet, "an oxcart. Then you can take me back to the village, boy." He gathered up his basket, put it on his head, and shoved by; and by the time Rama reached the cart, he was already tossing out some of the indigo leaves to make room for himself.

Rama cried out in dismay. "No, no, those are my indigo leaves for my mother's dye vats."

"Tut, tut, boy. I'll pay you an anna for your old weeds. Come along. I must be in the village by sundown." The juggler tossed another armful of the leaves out, shoved in his basket, and started to climb in himself. At that moment, however, he broke out, "Look, boy, look. There's a wild monkey in your cart here."

"She's not wild...." Rama broke off abruptly, remembering what had happened just that morning.

"Ah," the old man peered up at Moti, then back down at Rama. "That is the little imp who stole my turban this morning."

"She was only playing."

"Does she bite?"

Rama hesitated. "Only people who try to hurt her," he said, then added quickly, "she does all sorts of tricks, and all the children play with her."

"Well, look at her now."

Rama peered into the cart; and to tell the truth, Moti, with her teeth drawn back in a snarl, looked anything but a pet.

"She smells the cobra in your basket," Rama excused her.

"Cobra! I have no cobra in my basket, boy," the old man exploded. "I carry only a few scarfs and things for the magic I do in the village tonight."

"Well, then she smells the cobra you carried in the basket yesterday." Rama spoke stubbornly. "You can't fool Moti."

"Let's get along," the juggler said grumpily. He heaved himself up into the back of the cart and Rama, unwillingly, went around and climbed up in front. Moti came down and put her arms about his neck, but kept her wary little face peering over his shoulder at the stranger behind. And after a time Rama heard the juggler shifting up over the leaves, closer to him. "Nice little monkey," he heard him coaxing; but the next moment, as Moti nipped at him, he cried out, "Ouch! you evil imp!"

Rama pulled the monkey down in front of him, scolding her soundly. He looked around to say he was sorry, but the old juggler spoke in an oily tone.

"You're a fine big strong lad—the weaver's son, didn't they say?" he began.

Rama shook his head. "I was born a weaver's son; but, alas, I will never weave. No one weaves any more in our village but my mother, and she, only when someone asks her to make something for a wedding, as the baker's wife..."

"Then what are you going to do to get your rice?"

"Oh, I have the oxcart," Rama said happily. "Sometimes I drive the villagers across the plain to visit their relatives in the other villages. Sometimes I work in the paddy fields. Some day," his face brightened, "if we can save enough to buy another cow, we will sell the milk and I can go to the new school...."

"Oho!" the old man's eyes were blazing now. "You would go to school, eh? You a weaver's son—born with the fingers for a loom, yet you would use them instead to write with the pen like a babu. Why can't you be what the Creator meant you to be—a weaver?"

He edged closer, poked a long bony finger in Rama's face. "Mark my words, weaver's son, you'll end up like the black crow."

"Black crow?" Rama shrank back, stammering.

"Yes, the black crow. Haven't you ever heard of it? The black crow who wanted to be a white swan like the one floating on the lake. So he left his fine nest in the mango tree by the paddy field, spent the whole day wading up and down the water's edge washing his feathers,

waiting for them to turn white. But what happened?"
He poked his finger again. "He got thinner and thinner.
His feathers began to drop out, and then one day they
found him—*dead*—and still just an old black crow."

Rama did not answer. There was no use arguing with
old people, he knew. The juggler sounded just like
Grandmother whenever he and his mother started to
talk about school.

"Why do you, a weaver's son, want to go to school?"
the juggler demanded.

"I would like to write letters and figures...."

"What for?" the old man had quite a wild look in
his eyes now. "So you can sit in a hot little room in the
big city and count how much gold is in the Rajah's
strongboxes?"

"No, no," Rama said with sudden spirit, "they are
going to teach lots of other things in the new school.
They are going to teach us how to grow grass on the
plain here, and how to grow pumpkins as big as my head,
and how to get twenty baskets of rice from our strip of
land instead of one—we have just one strip...."

"Aha," the juggler said slyly, "but have they told you
that they are going to take that one strip of land away
from you, and those twenty baskets of rice will go into
the Rajah's storehouse? And that they are going to put
a fence all around that part of the plain where that green

grass is to grow so that your buffaloes or your ox can't get at it? No, no." He turned, shook his fist in a frenzy up toward the sky, "No, it's all to be kept for this foreign flying cow. *The foreign cow.* The plain that the Creator gave for our own sacred Hindu cows."

Rama's big brown eyes grew bigger. "The whole plain, fenced in? But where will my ox find grass then? And where will Dumbir drive his water buffaloes?"

"And have they told you," the juggler waxed more violent when he saw how he was scaring Rama, "that they are going to make the villagers keep all their cattle out of the lanes, keep them tied up in their own court-yards?"

"But how will they find food then? Oh no, you are not speaking the truth, juggler," Rama began to argue; but suddenly seeing the strange look in the juggler's eyes, he broke off abruptly and hurried his ox on faster toward the village.

But the juggler was determined to talk. "And about this cow that's flying down here," he shouted. "You know why the Rajah is bringing it here, don't you? He's going to get rid of all our sacred Hindu cows and bring in these foreign ones from across the seas." He broke off, moaning a prayer, *Ram-Ram-Ram.*

Rama's eyes were rolling in horror. He had been brought up to believe that the cow was the most sacred of all animals. The big village bull had his horns painted gold and fresh garlands of flowers put on his neck each morning. The baker beat his breast when the huge sleek fellow came trampling down his cakes; the women wailed when he foraged in their gardens; but no one dared ever drive him off or lift a stick to him. As to the little village cows, they were a poor, starved, dirty lot, feeding on garbage or the scant grass of the plain. They were left to die alone when old or sick. Still, they were sacred, and only by treating them as such could a good Hindu hope to reach heaven.

The juggler was pounding on the indigo leaves now and shouting, "Yes, and it's happening all over our land. These wicked men who have gone to foreign schools now come back to make us do as these foreigners do. But I, for one..." he raised his bony arm high, fist clenched, "I have made a vow that I will destroy every one of these foreign cows I find. I swear it with my life." At this he sank back exhausted and closed his eyes, seeming to be in some sort of a trance.

Rama urged the bullock on faster. The village was still a long way off, though he could see the broken head on the old Buddha temple that lay just outside it rising up against the sky. Suddenly, though, he caught a sound that made him stop, frowning.

"What's up?" the juggler called out.

But Rama was already out of the cart, scythe in hand. "I hear a cow—back here in the cactus—a cow's caught back in here. . . ."

"So a cow's caught back in the cactus . . . *Ram-Ram-Ram!* What of it?" The old juggler, peering out around the back of the cart, spat on the ground. "When do we get to the village, boy?"

Rama's face looked troubled. "She's lost," he said talking now to himself more than to the old man, "Dumbir never brings his herds out to this part of the plain near the Black Oil Pool. She's stuck in it, most likely. It sounds as though she's hurt."

"Dolt! Dolt! No wonder you drive such a rickety old cart, boy! We'll never get to the village if we stop for every bawling cow. Leave the cow in the mud, boy. I've got to get to the village to put my show on before it's dark."

But Rama was already hacking his way in through the thorns, and did not hear. Nor did he see the old man climb out, yank his basket after him, and start muttering on his way on foot.

III   The Magic Circle

"*Ram-Ram-Ram!* However did you get in here?" Rama almost laughed when he finally came on the cow, caught fast by a bit of frayed rope around a cactus clump. He had never seen a dirtier, funnier-looking little animal, coated as she was in black, oily mud and matted with tiny green burrs even to her eyelashes. She had her eyes closed against the myriad of flies swarming around them. Her head was uplifted, and she was keeping up the frantic bawling. At the sound of Rama's voice, though, she rolled big pathetic eyes around at him, gave a last feeble *moo*, and grew quiet. She reached out a long, rough, parched tongue and licked his arm.

Rama hacked away the cactus and in another moment

she was following him eagerly out to the road. He made her fast to the back of the cart and then, with a worried, "Now we've got to get these indigo leaves back to Grandmother," he once more started on his way. And it was only when he heard Moti, no longer wary, jibbering out at the cow from the back of the cart that he realized he had lost his unfriendly passenger.

He thought ruefully of the lost anna, of his wilted leaves. He wondered what he was to do with the cow. Should he turn her loose in the village, or keep her tied up in the courtyard till the herdboy came looking for her?

The cow settled the question herself when they finally came to the dried river bed which ran between the plain and the village. Rama felt her give a tug and peered out to see her, heels and tail high in the air, gaily skipping off through the sand, disappearing in among some reeds.

He sighed. His home lay just ahead on the opposite bank, and Moti had already hurried across. But the sun had dropped into the plain, and in another hour the hyena and cheetah would be out. "No, I can't leave that cow out here," he told himself and patiently turned the ox down the river bed.

A good thing, too, for the next moment Dumbir came racing by in a cloud of dust with his buffaloes. He shouted out something about the Rajah and the juggler, but his words were lost in all the noise.

Rama found the cow standing knee-deep in a muddy pool, choking on the dirty water. She refused to budge. "Come, bossy, come," he coaxed, "the hyena is coming." He grew more anxious when he saw how she was beginning to bloat up and breathe heavily. He ran his hands down over her, noticing for the first time what a nice plump animal she was. Odd looking, with no hump like the other village cows, but with a fine big udder which would soon fill many milk bowls.

Rama's big dark eyes were beginning to sparkle. What if the cow didn't belong to anyone in the village? What if she was part of some bride's dowry, broken loose from the back of the cart carrying her to a distant village, and given up as dead? He recalled one of his grandmother's stories about her uncle who had found such a cow, been allowed to keep it by the village council, and had built up a fortune on it. What if he could keep this one! He would sell the milk for an anna a bowl. He could already see himself at the next Durga festival giving his mother that fine new brass pot she wanted; and a warm blanket for grandmother; and for himself a white shirt and Gandhi cap such as the schoolboys wore—for of course he would go to school now.

"Come on, bossy!" he shouted so gaily that the cow came to life and allowed herself to be dragged from the pool. He led her warily down the river bed to the deserted part of the village which had not been rebuilt since the last flood, the ox following behind, and turned her into the old cattle yard at the far end of his grandmother's mustard field. When he turned to leave, though, the cow came after him, bawling loudly as though to say, *I am not going to be left alone.*

Rama looked around, troubled, then ran out, pulled an armful of grass from the bundle hanging under the cart, and brought it back in to her. He left her happily munching, as, after making fast the old gate, he hurried on his way.

At sundown the big mango tree cast a pleasant shade over the weaver's courtyard and the little mud house with its palm-leaf roof. The purple of the bougainvillea mingled with the gold of the marigolds and the green of the sacred tulasi tree. There was a happy gurgle of water in the old stone sluice which ran in from the well to the dye vat. The big loom with the almost-finished blanket on it stood up against the wall. Rama's mother, pretty and young though she wore a white widow's sari, was kneeling on a mat pounding out green and red chilis. Rama sniffed at the tempting odor of pea soup.

Grandmother made haste to unload the indigo leaves and began stripping the leaves for the vat. "A small load for such a long day," she grumbled. But his mother jumped up to ask eagerly, "Did you hear anything about the flying cow, son?"

Rama had quite forgotten the flying cow. Before he could reply however she went on, "Everyone's been talking about it all day out at the well. And Dumbir just went by with his buffaloes. He said he saw it. He actually saw it."

"You mean it isn't here yet?"

"The Rajah is still out there on the plain waiting for it."

"Well, you may be sure Dumbir will see it first," Grandmother put in wryly. "I wouldn't believe that boy, not if I saw him flying in on the cow himself."

"No." Rama's mother shook her head. "I believe Dumbir somehow this time."

Rama's eyes were big with fear. "What did he say it looked like? Why didn't it come down to the Rajah? Where was it?"

"Over by the teakwoods. He had just driven the buffaloes into the pool there—it was at high noon—when he saw this great monster." His mother's eyes were as big as Rama's now; and, because she was a timid little woman, her voice shook with fear. "He said it had a huge, fat body, great silver wings and a long tail flowing out like the dancer's veil. It was spitting out smoke and fire from underneath...."

"You don't really believe that Dumbir saw all that," Grandmother put in scornfully. "You don't believe him when he tells how he has pulled a cheetah off his buffalo's back, or how he saw a snake as long as the palm tree...."

"Yes, but the boy was trembling today. I saw that myself," Mother insisted.

"I'm going to run up to the bazaar and hear the news," Rama broke in.

Any other night Grandmother would have said firmly, "Oh, no, you're not. You are going to take the ox back to the pool and bathe it. And you are going to eat your rice...." But tonight it was plain everything in the little village was topsy-turvy, and they were not sorry to have someone get the news for them. Rama, in fact, did hear her calling angrily after him, but, thinking she was ordering him back, did not turn. He understood a few minutes later as he ran through one of the narrow lanes and saw Moti skipping along the wall top alongside him.

"Ah, you nuisance," Rama groaned. This was one time he did not wish to be bothered with his pet. Moti always found some mischief to be up to in the bazaar.

He had no time to catch her and take her back though; so, hoping for the best, he hurried on through the maze of little lanes that led out to the bazaar.

"Something's up all right," he told himself when he saw the crowd. A juggler, a traveling show, always brought out almost everyone in the little village that lay in the heart of the plain, miles from even the railway station, cut off from the big outside world. Tonight, one group jammed in front of the Rajah's gates and the new school on one side, others around the banyan tree over by the village shrine. In between milled the buffaloes and goats, snorting and bawling, knocking over the merchants' stalls while their herdboys gaped.

There were all sorts of rumors going around. Dumbir's story was being repeated by many. All were wondering why the Rajah had not returned with the now-fabulous cow. Something terrible had happened it was whispered; and one old woman had said openly that probably the monster had devoured them all. The younger people laughed at this.

Rama drank in all this, then pushed on across to the banyan tree. And once again, above the din, he caught the weird notes of the juggler's flute. He tried to push through, but the crowd was too great. He edged around, far back in under the hanging roots of the old tree, pulled himself up to one of the branches, and crept out

to a spot where, hidden well by the leaves, he could look down on the juggler. He let out an angry "Hush" when he heard Moti's familiar *beep-beep* just above him. By now it was almost dark.

The juggler had drawn a large white circle on the ground and was now sitting cross-legged on a reed mat in the center of it, basket beside him. He was wearing a voluminous yellow wide-sleeved robe. He had smeared his face with paint, drawn great white circles about his eyes, and painted the eyelids blue so that now he had quite a ghostly appearance. His eyes were closed, and his bony fingers moved slowly up and down the reed, mesmerizing the crowd with the monotonous high notes as he would have a cobra.

"Come on, old fakir," someone called out crossly, "let's see your cobra dance."

The juggler's eyes opened wide. He turned the basket upside down to show its emptiness and shouted, "I'm not a snake charmer. I make magic with a dry mango seed, make the tree grow in five minutes."

"Then why play the snake flute?"

The people laughed, and some moved off to the Rajah's gate. But most of them crowded in closer. Fakirs had been doing this mango-tree trick for centuries in the little village, but it never ceased to awe. Nor indeed could anyone ever explain it.

"Back, villagers, back," the juggler ordered. "If you cross that white line my tree will not have room to grow."

The crowd pushed back. The juggler closed his eyes, spread out his hands, and began to intone a prayer in some strange language. Then, looking up, eyes grown large and luminous, after showing his hands to be empty, he magically brought a knife out of the air and with it dug a deep narrow hole in the clay. Chanting another prayer he produced a green silk scarf out of nowhere, from which he took out an ordinary dried mango seed. He planted it and covered it with earth. Chanting again he brought down a red silk scarf, covered the spot, and then pulled it off to show a tiny green shoot already sprouting. The crowd cried *ah* admiringly. And now the juggler began intoning again. He sat back, eyes glazed like one in a trance, waiting, passing his bony hands with their loose, flapping, wide sleeves back and forth, till he had the crowd waiting breathless. They knew the routine perfectly. The next scarf would be bright yellow; and when he lifted it, the sprig would have grown into a tiny tree bearing a mango blossom.

The juggler began his chant. And up in the tree above Rama let out a groan, for a moment before he had seen Moti drop to the ground and creep up close to the juggler's basket. The little mischief was drawing something out from under the juggler's robe. A bright yellow silk scarf. She rose, jibbering, shook it out even as the juggler did, and looked curiously at the mango tree fastened securely to the one side of it. The juggler went on chanting, groping too, but for once the magic scarf refused to flip down out of the air. And suddenly, as the crowd began to howl with laughter, he looked around and saw what the monkey was doing. With a cry of rage he lunged back and tried to seize the scarf; but Moti had already disappeared up into the tree with it.

The crowd waited for the outburst that must surely follow; but to their surprise the old man rose, smiling. "Did you, villagers," he cried out, "really think I could make a dried mango seed blossom into a tree in five minutes? How could I? It took the great Creator many hundreds of years to make this…" he pointed up at the banyan tree "…grow from a tiny seed. Then why should I, a mere man, think I could grow one in five minutes? Why, even the little wild monkey knew better than that. She knew I was just tricking you. She came down to see how it was done." The old man suddenly dropped his smooth manner. His eyes began to blaze and his tone rose high and far-reaching. "Are your wits duller than those of a monkey, villagers? Listen to me."

The people came crowding in close now, even from across at the Rajah's gate. They stood silent as the juggler went on, the flickering torches, since it was now dark, casting eerie shadows over his face.

"Can't you see how your Rajah is tricking you? All this talk about changing the plain into pasture land, growing rice in the sand where the Creator meant only the cobra and ant to feed. Promising you ten sers of rice from your strip of land which can now grow only one. Bah, bah, bah! What rot!" He paused for breath then went on with still greater feeling. "And about this foreign cow. You don't think the Rajah is going to grow grass on the plain for our poor sacred Hindu cows, do you? He has already fenced off great chunks of it. He has already ordered you to get your cows off the streets, keep them tied in your own courtyards. He is now planting foreign seed to grow the special grain this precious foreign cow must have to eat. Soon, if you don't want to see your own village cows lying dead by the roadside, you will be forced to buy foreign food that comes in bags."

"Buy food for our cows?" Everyone looked stunned.

"So, villagers," the juggler's voice rose high, "are you going to let this foreign cow come in and destroy our sacred Hindu ones?"

"Put a curse on it, holy man. Put a curse on it," an old woman shouted and they all took up the cry.

"That's not right," a young man tried to make himself heard. He was wearing the white shirt and Gandhi cap of the new school. "The Rajah is bringing in the foreign cow to start a healthier breed in our village. Just as we sent some of our fine Brahma bulls across the seas to their land a few years ago to start a breed that could live on their plains."

"Ah!" someone shouted out. "So that is where our fine bulls all went. No wonder our babies have no milk!"

"A curse on the foreign cow!" they all began again. "Put a curse on the beast, fakir!"

"It's up to you to do that," the juggler urged. "Rise up, villagers! Destroy the evil thing! Destroy it before

41

it destroys your sacred Hindu village. If you don't…"
But at this point he faltered, for, emerging suddenly
out from the darkness between the hanging roots behind,
was the Rajah's big elephant.

With only a faint tinkle of bells it stepped into the
juggler's magic circle.

IV   The Flying Cow Is Lost

They all—the Rajah, his little daughter, the mahout,
the elephant even—looked tired and dusty. It was clear
they had had a long, hard day out on the plain.

The Rajah stood up in the howdah and pointed down
at the juggler. "You juggle with words better than you
do with your mango tree, trickster," he cried out. He
looked at the villagers. "And you who are shouting
'a curse on the flying cow!'—well, it looks as though
your curse has worked. The poor little foreign cow
that was coming to your village to give milk for your
babies, perhaps she felt the hatred awaiting her—I don't
know—but it is not likely she will come now to trouble
you. She is more likely lying dead at this very moment
out in the jungle."

"Dead in the jungle! Oh, no, no, no. What happened?" Now there was a great outcry from the many villagers who had been waiting to welcome the flying cow.

"Well, something has happened to the airplane, we fear," the Rajah began.

Airplane. Rama, hanging low to catch every word, almost fell from the tree. He was tingling with excitement. He had never seen one of those wonderful things for they seldom passed over the village; and, when they did, shot like silver arrows, so fast and so high that no one could tell what they were like. But he had seen pictures of them in the newspapers which came wrapped around the merchant's bales of cloth. He was so thrilled now at the thought of seeing one actually in the village that he did not even notice Moti dropping like a little shadow, scarf still in hand, into the big howdah again. He strained to catch what the Rajah was saying.

"We fear it has had an accident, has fallen into the jungle. That means our little cow is gone." Suddenly breaking into a rage, the Rajah turned and pointed again at the juggler. "And there you stand, you evil mischief-maker—one who makes a business of going from place to place stirring up mischief—you stand there planning to undo the good we are trying to bring to our village. All the rest of India is waking up. They

44

are building homes and canals and schools for their children, roads for motor cars, fertilizing their land, raising new strains of cattle that will give enough milk to keep their babies healthy. But we—look at us here, still wallowing through the mud in oxcarts as our fathers did a thousand years ago. Our children can't read, they can't write. They have only a handful of rice a day. Shame on us! And shame on you, old fakir, in your filthy rags, daring to come here ranting about our sacred cows! Sacred! Look at the poor starved creatures wandering about looking for refuse. No, no, no! The Creator never meant animals nor children to look like ours!"

The villagers stood awed by the Rajah's words and manner.

But he was going on, speaking more quietly now. "This little foreign cow was something very special. She was bought and raised by a group of farm boys and girls in America. She took many prizes at their village fairs. She was their best. And they sent her as a token of friendship, as a gift to our village. But..." he broke off, looking very tired. "I tell you now what I want. There is just a chance that the airplane has fallen down somewhere near here on the plain. The men who were driving it, the pilots, and the little cow may still be alive. But they will not be by morning. We must move fast. Go, get your donkeys, your horses, your work-elephants, your torches! Form into groups and go, search the plain."

"Dumbir, the herdboy, can tell you which way it went," someone shouted out excitedly. "He saw it. He saw it!"

"A herdboy saw it! Where is he?" Everyone was excited now.

Dumbir was pushed forward. He began telling the strange tale he had told Rama's mother about seeing a monster with great silver wings, spitting fire out of its belly; but the Rajah stopped him with an impatient, "No, no, boy, that wasn't the cow. That was the airplane. Where did you see this? Quick, quick, boy. Where were you when it passed?"

"I was over by the teakwoods near the Buddha temple. I had just taken my buffaloes..."

But the Rajah broke in again with, "Here, boy, you must come along with us and show us exactly where you were and in which direction the plane was going." The next moment the dazed Dumbir found himself, at the mahout's order to the elephant, being lifted up in a big trunk and dropped back down into the howdah. There Moti, who had been putting the juggler's gay scarf about the little Kamala's neck, let out a scream and leaped back up into the tree.

The Rajah gave a few last words to the crowd about the cow. "She looks just like any of our village ones, only plumper and better kept. And she has no hump. And short curved horns. She seems to be frisky but she is really very gentle and will come if you call her name. She has a pale gold coat and a wide black face, not narrow like our cows."

"What is her name?" they cried.

"Peppy. Her name is Peppy."

"A strange name that. Peppy...." The word rippled through the crowd. *Peppy* . . . *Peppy* . . . *Peppy*. . . .

"It means—full of pepper—red-hot peppers." The Rajah smiled faintly. "But she is very gentle. So get started, villagers. And we will fire off the big cannon to let you know when she is found. And, of course..."

But Rama did not wait to hear the rest. He was already out of the banyan tree, racing for home.

V   The Flying Cow Is Found

Rama sped through the now-moonlit lanes, the monkey skipping along on the wall tops beside him. When he came to his own home he stopped and peeped in through the gate. Grandmother was standing in the shadow by the wall stirring the dye vat. His mother was taking off her finished cloth from the loom. He crept on down the lane, across the mustard field, into the old pen. Then, breathing hard, he stood staring at the little cow happily chewing her cud over in the far corner.

"Peppy!" he brought the word out in a whisper, hoping she would not respond.

But she did, and came running. She let out a welcoming *moo...oo* quite unlike the sniffing sound the village cows always made.

He pulled the burrs from her eyelids, took her wide face between his palms, and looked deep into her big dark eyes. He grabbed a handful of straw and rubbed a spot clean on the black, oily body. He ran his hand down the straight humpless back. Then said sadly, "Alas, Peppy, you are Peppy. And I must take you to the Rajah."

Feeling very sad now he took the frayed rope and led her outside. But the moment she was in the lane she gave a great tug and, with heels high in the air, was racing for the river bed. He followed panting. He found her back in the pool in the reeds again. She rolled a roguish eye at him, cried a happy *moo,* and licked his arm.

"No, Peppy," he cried in distress, "you can't stay here. You've got to go to the palace."

But Peppy had made up her mind. She also had strong legs and she stood firm now in the mud. This was the first cool spot she had found in India, and the night wind was just beginning to blow. Rama found a bit of broken pot and began to scoop up water, pouring it over her. She closed her eyes blissfully and let out a *moo* for more. The caked black mud was beginning to ooze off, letting streaks of pale gold hide show through. He took a handful of reed and began to scrub vigorously.

His eyes glowed as the face emerged velvety soft and black, the body sleek, satiny gold. He put his arms about her and rested his face against hers, murmuring, "Ah but you are beautiful, Peppy. And meant for the Rajah's stable. Not even our village bull is as fine as you and..."

But at this point Moti, who had followed and had been sitting in the sand watching curiously, let out a warning *beep-beep* and disappeared back into the reeds for safety. Rama turned and found the juggler standing just behind. "So you found the flying cow, eh, weaver's boy? Humph!" he said. He drew closer to examine her.

"Yes," Rama burst out eagerly, "and she isn't a monster at all as you said, juggler. See, she is just like our own cows, only cleaner and plumper and she is very gentle and she wants to be friends."

But the juggler was not listening. His eyes were beginning to take on that bright wild look again. He muttered, as to himself, "So this is one of the foreign cows—whose vile blood is to mingle with that of our sacred Hindu ones! Whose vile foreign milk is to be fed to our Hindu babies! No, no, *no!* It must not be!" He reached out for the rope, but Rama seized it and drew the cow back.

The juggler shook his head as though to clear it.

Changing his tone as quickly as he did his scarfs he spoke in an oily tone. "Here, boy, I am going back into the village. I'll take her for you."

But Rama tugged the cow further away. He was thinking of the juggler's angry threat under the banyan tree, *I will destroy every foreign cow I find.* "No," he said bravely, "I will take her in myself."

The juggler's eyes narrowed. "You are a sly one, weaver's boy," he spat out. He pointed up the river bed where the hollow *clackety-clockety* of the work-elephants' bells could be heard, and the flares of the villagers seen as they hurried for the plain. "Anyone could see through you. You plan to keep the cow hidden till the reward grows bigger, eh? The longer the search the more rupees."

Rama did not understand such words. The juggler reached out to take the rope again and said threateningly now, "But you will be smarter to let me take the

cow in. You see, I know how you found it out on the plain today. I was watching here from the reeds when you took it in by the back lanes and hid it in your own goat yard. You hoped it would be given up for dead and then you could claim it as your own."

Rama's eyes were big with fear. The old juggler certainly did have some magic power since he could read even what a boy was thinking.

"Yes, yes," the old fellow was going on now, "just think of all the trouble you would have saved our poor, tired, hungry Rajah—waiting out there on the plain all day—if you had just taken the animal straight in when you found it. And what of that poor teakwood cutter who was thrown from the elephant while searching the jungle today for the cow. He would not be lying dead tonight. Alas, alas, weaver's boy, I fear you are in for a lot of trouble." The bony old hand was almost on the rope now.

But at this point Peppy let out a terrible bawl, lowered her head, and charged at the juggler, who tumbled out of the way crying, "Why, the evil beast! The evil beast!"

"It's that smell of cobra on you, juggler," Rama said earnestly. "Or else she sees the hate in your eyes."

"And I tell you," the juggler's voice fairly shook with rage, "I have no cobra on me." He pointed his bony finger at Rama. "You take the ugly brute to the Rajah yourself. But the curses of Durga, and Ganesh, and all our other Hindu gods be on you for touching the foreign thing!"

But Rama was already hurrying the cow up out of the river bed.

She grew quite unruly, though, when they started through the narrow mud-walled lanes. She shied at the shadows and at Moti flitting along the wall tops beside them, and sniffed at the strange smells. It took constant coaxing, "Come on, Peppy, come on," and gentle stroking to get her as far as the bazaar.

Usually it was crowded on a moonlit night but now it was deserted save for a few buffaloes and goats left by lazy herdboys. There was no one under the banyan tree making a speech, no women filling their waterpots at the tank. The little white temple lay mirrored in its still waters. There was only one old watchman, Alwar, at the Rajah's gate.

Rama tugged the cow up to him. Grandmother, who was a great storyteller, was always talking of the days when guards in smart red uniforms and high turbans, swords at side, had stood at that spot. A cannon had fired a salute every time the Rajah passed. Silver bugles had announced the dawn and the sunset. The big gates in the high white wall of the Rani's palace had never been open. Nor indeed had any of the women been seen with faces uncovered. Now the gates were never shut. And Kamala, the Rajah's only daughter—so old villagers groaned—went to school with the boys and was running wild, climbing trees just like the outcastes who belonged outside the village wall.

But the Rajah's garden with its playing fountains and rose beds and green lawn was just as lovely as it had been back in Grandmother's day. Peppy was already sniffing at it. Before Rama could explain, though, the old watchman was crying out, "Off with you, herdboy! Take your cow from the Rajah's gate." He raised his stick, and Peppy, insulted, lowered her head and charged forward just as she had at the juggler. "Off with you, boy," Alwar roared.

Rama tugged the cow down the road and then stood wondering what to do with her. Peppy knew, though, and with another lunge she tore loose and back into the garden. Alwar had disappeared.

Rama raced after her, whispering frantically, "Peppy! Peppy! Peppy!" But by now she was just a pale blob flitting in and out between the shrubs. Every time he neared her she looked around roguishly, kicked her heels and went gamboling on. *Splash,* through the fountain, trailing lotus blossoms after her. *Snip, snap, snip.* Rama groaned as he heard the branches and stems going down beneath her hoofs. He was hot and tired and angry and about to give up, when finally he came on her, back in the shadow close to the wall, lying down, fast asleep. He tugged at her, trying to get her up, but she did not move even an eyelash. And, hearing the watchman nearby, he decided he too had better lie low for a time. He huddled down close beside her. Moti came edging in alongside. In another moment all three were fast asleep.

He was wakened by a whack from a bamboo stick. "Out of here, herdboy! How dare you bring your cow in here?" the watchman was roaring. Rama struggled up, ducking the blows; then, fully awake as he saw the cow disappearing off across the flower beds toward the street, he raced after her, crying, "Stop her. Stop her. It's the flying cow!" By the time he had reached the gate she had gone. "Which way did she go?" he called frantically to a lone figure wrapped in a blanket, standing nearby.

"Who?" It was Dumbir, looking very sleepy and cross, making his way home alone, and on foot.

"The flying cow, Dumbir. I found her. But she's run away again...."

But at the words *flying cow* Dumbir had come to life. He began to run. Rama raced after him, but lost him under the hanging roots of the banyan tree. And while he stood, listening, wondering which way to go, the big cannon over in the Rajah's tower suddenly boomed out.

Peppy, the flying cow, had been found.

VI   Moti and Peppy

Rama, sleeping out in the courtyard on a reed mat, stirred, unrolled himself from his cloth, and sat up blinking. The big morning star was hanging low in a still-black sky; but the ox over in the lean-to by the house was bawling, and there was a gurgle of water in the sluice behind that told him his grandmother had already been out to the well. And now he could hear the gentle *swish swish* of the paddle as she stirred the dye in the vat, getting it ready for the new blanket.

Over in the cooking room he could see his mother lighting the little oil wick in the niche in the wall, placing a marigold before her household mud god.

"Hurry, son," Grandmother called out, "you must water the ox. We have hired the cart out for the day to the merchant. And you had better get out to the paddy field fast. Those thieving birds were terrible yesterday. We won't have a ser left for the storehouse unless we do something."

Rama made haste to twist on his turban, which he had been using as a blanket during the night. He ran out to the well. Dawn comes early in India, and a faint pink was already showing in the sky. Women with waterpots were already clustered around gossiping about the strange happenings of the night. He caught the words "Dumbir" and "flying cow."

"And just think it was our brave Dumbir who found it," someone was saying, "Fancy him riding up on the Rajah's elephant with the little Rani. I still don't believe it."

"Well, my husband was there and saw it," the baker's wife spoke up, "Dumbir took them out, showed them where he had seen the airplane..."

"The flying cow, you mean."

There was a general titter at this, for by now Dumbir's mistake, taking the airplane for the cow itself, had become a joke.

"...but then," the baker's wife went on, "he got sleepy, and the Rajah let him out and told him to go on home with one of the teakwood cutters. On his way over to a work-elephant, though, he heard the cow crying back in the jungle...."

"In the jungle! Ah!" The women all exclaimed at this, for no one ever dared venture into the jungle alone at night.

"Yes," Dumbir's sister took up the story, "and just as he got there a cheetah was about to spring on her— he had a terrible time getting her out...."

Any other time the women would have laughed and said "Oho, another of Dumbir's cheetah stories." But this morning, with the flying cow safely housed in the Rajah's stable, they could say nothing.

"Well," an old woman mumbled, "it looks as though our Dumbir is really as brave as he says he is."

No, no, no, he's lying, Rama wanted to shout out; but, remembering the juggler's warning that he would get into trouble over keeping the cow hidden, he stood silent now.

And at that moment a boy shouted out, "But where is this airplane they said was coming down to our village?"

"Oh," the baker's wife took up the story gladly, "the Rajah found it later over in that village which lies on the far side of the teakwood forest. Something went wrong with it when it was up in the sky. Smoke came out of it, and the driver had to bring it down fast. They pulled out the cow, tied her to a tree while they were finding the trouble, and when they looked around she was gone."

"Probably flew on by herself," the old woman muttered.

No one paid attention to her, though, and the talk went back to Dumbir.

"Where is our brave herdboy this morning?" someone asked. "And his buffaloes?"

"Probably trampling down my pumpkins at this very moment."

"Dumbir won't need to be driving buffaloes to the plain any more. He will be riding in the Rajah's howdah, and his family will grow fat on the rupees the Rajah will give him for finding the cow...."

They all began to argue about the reward Dumbir was sure to get. Some thought he would be given a fine post in the palace. Fifty rupees someone else said. No, a hundred at least, the merchant put in. The cow was worth many thousands of gold pieces he had heard.

At this point, however, the old juggler, who had come up unnoticed, cried out, "I can tell you what reward the herdboy will get."

"Tell us then, juggler, since you can read the Rajah's mind," the merchant cried out wryly.

"He'll give the herdboy a white shirt, put a Gandhi cap on his head, give him a slate and a pencil, and put him in his new school, where he will learn how to use a foreign plow, how to build foreign fences around your plain, how to grow foreign grass for his fine cow —so the Rajah can get more milk to bring in more rupees to put in his strong boxes; so he can send his sons across the seas to learn more foreign ways...." He broke off, took his big basket from his head, plumped it down on the ground, and prepared to start out on another speech. "Oh, you fools! You simple village bumpkins! Can't you see through this Rajah of yours?"

"As we saw your mango tree last night, old fakir?" an urchin called out saucily.

Everyone laughed, and the crowd began to break up. The wheel started creaking at the well, the women filling their pots. Rama, fearing the juggler's eyes, crept out of sight.

He stopped in dismay when he saw one of the Rajah's servants standing at his own gate, talking to Grandmother. "Alas," he groaned, "they have come to arrest me for hiding the cow."

But at that moment the servant, spotting him, cried out, "Ah, there you are, son. I'm here looking for nice clean rice-straw, free of thorns, for the Rajah's new stable. I see you have some. I'll give you six annas a load for it."

"He'll bring a load right away," Grandmother put in quickly.

"The foreign cow fares better than our own poor," the juggler's wry voice broke in from behind.

"Not if the Rajah has his way," the servant replied. "He plans to have all the village cows eating proper food and sleeping on clean straw like the foreign one. He has already bought five of the moneylender's old bony ones and put them in stalls alongside the new one. They will be bedded and fed the same as the new one, and the villagers will see then what can be done with their cattle."

"Our Hindu cows have managed to live since time began on the grass of the plain, which the Creator meant for them."

"And our babies have been dying for lack of milk...." The servant, aware that the old man was out to argue, broke off and turned to Rama. "All right, boy, bring a load along to the new stable, down behind the school. Make sure it's well tied, though. Anand, who cares for the stable, won't have a loose straw on his clean floor. And say I sent you." With that he went on his way, the juggler after him.

Rama, with Grandmother and Mother both helping, hastened to tie up a great load of the rice-straw and shifted it up on his head. Then, after calling out, "Keep Moti tied up in the shed, be sure!" he started off at a jog trot down the lane, smiling happily at the thought of the six annas soon to be knotted in his turban end. He let out a groan, though, when, after just a few steps, he heard Moti's familiar *beep-beep*, and she came grinning up alongside, broken cord trailing from her loins. There was nothing he could do about it though, with the big load on his head. So he trotted on, hoping for once that the monkey would disappear into the bazaar to pester the merchants while he took his straw into the stable.

He forgot Moti, however, when he came close to the school and saw a crowd gathered around the gate. The old watchman was ordering the juggler to move on.

"Just listen to that." A woman turned to Rama, shocked. "They are driving a poor old pilgrim from the Rajah's gate just because he carries the cobra basket with him. Who ever heard of such a thing before? Don't we pray to the cobra, put rice and flowers before his hole? Won't he punish us for this insult? Haven't we been brought up to give alms—not blows—to the pilgrim?"

"They are not giving blows," a student explained. "They are just asking the juggler to put his show on across the bazaar, where the cows won't hear his flute. Cows won't give down their milk when they know a cobra is near."

"Then the cobra-god did not mean us to have the milk," the woman cried out.

"I tell you I don't carry a cobra," the juggler shouted, "I carry only some scarfs."

"With a mango tree growing on one."

The crowd laughed, and parted to let the juggler pass through. Rama made his way timidly down the long croton-bordered road with the new school on one side and the Rajah's high white wall on the other. He paused to listen—*ah, what a fine sound it was*—to the students chanting out their letters. He looked around troubled when, during a lull, from the other side he heard a shrill voice calling "Come, Moti, come, Moti! Come!"

Kamala, face streaked with dirt, skirt torn, shreds of leaf clinging to her pigtails, and looking as though she had just tumbled from a tree, was standing in a narrow gateway, holding up a big red mango and coaxing, "Come, Moti, come, Moti!" The monkey was nowhere in sight.

But at that moment he heard a familiar *moo* that

started his heart pounding and sent him hurrying on.

Peppy, the flying cow, was standing out in front of the new barn, the Rajah and a group of students ringed around her. Rama was bursting with pride, just as though she belonged to him. And in a certain way she did. But now, in the morning sun, after a good rest, another bath and much currycombing, wearing a new red halter, she was indeed a thing of beauty.

The Rajah was explaining, in words so simple that even Rama could understand, why the foreign cow had such a satiny coat and such straight legs, and why she would give such rich milk when her little calf arrived.

Rama's eyes opened wide at that.

"It is a great shame," the Rajah was saying now, "that in this India of ours, where we have more cattle than any other country of the world, we have less milk for our babies. And that is not because our cows are a poorer breed, nor because we do not have enough land. It is simply because we are not making proper use of what we have. Now I am going to take you on into our experimental room and show you what we plan to do. We have taken five village cows in and are going to give each one a different feed for the next three months. Some will have corn added to their grass, some vitamins. (There were many words now which Rama did not understand; still he stood drinking them all in.) Each cow will be weighed each day, and in that way we will find out which food is best suited for the ones in this part of India. I am going to show you too how to care for the milk." He turned to a man in a white coat and cap nearby and called out, "You can take Peppy back into the barn, Anand."

He handed the end of the halter out, but Peppy, who had been standing quietly through all the demonstration, evidently quite used to such things, suddenly gave a loud *moo*, kicked up her heels, pulled loose, and headed for Rama. The students scattered in terror.

"Hold her, boy, hold her," the Rajah shouted, "she won't hurt you." He came running to seize her halter again. "She just smelled your nice fresh straw."

Under his big umbrella of straw Rama smiled broadly. *He does not know she knows me,* he told himself proudly.

"There, Anand." The Rajah handed the cow over to the keeper. He was laughing. "We are going to have to keep an eye on this little flying cow of ours. Your name suits you, you young scamp." He gave the cow a loving pat and led his class into the barn.

Rama longed to follow, but Anand was calling, "This way, boy." So he hurried on with his load, stacked it out in the yard, and came back in mopping his face to wait while the keeper went off to get the six annas.

He stood looking around him, awed. He had never been in such a grand place. The barn with its high teak-wood rafters, white-washed walls and many iron-barred windows, was cool and airy. Tools hung in orderly array in racks. The six cows stood, each in its own stall, before well-filled bins of hay, floors bedded with clean straw. Through the doorway beyond there was a glimpse of that magical place called Experimental Room—with gleaming machines, buckets, pans, bottles, books. And Anand bent over a desk, writing.

"Chase that monkey out of the barn, grass-boy," the keeper's voice roused him. "There's a monkey just run in."

Rama groaned. Even before he spotted the little pale gray nuisance up on the rafter over Peppy, he knew who it was. "Moti," he urged in whisper, "come on down, Moti. There's a good girl."

But Moti had suddenly let out a scream of terror and fled higher in the rafters. Now she was keeping up a shrill bark.

"What is it, Rama?" Kamala cried out from the doorway. "What is it?" She backed out as now Peppy and the other cows began to kick and tug.

Rama did not answer. He edged in alongside the cow, peered down into the bin, then cautiously loosed the halter rope and backed her out. Tugging her quickly across to Kamala he shoved the rope into her hand and choked out, "Get her out of here, quick. And hang on to her!" He grabbed at one of the forks on the wall and was running back into the stall when Anand's angry voice called out, "Whatever do you think you're doing, grass-boy?"

"And you, Kamala," the Rajah's voice, even more cross, broke in from behind. "What are you doing here?"

Rama looked around with white of eyes showing. "It's a snake—in the bin here—Moti never screams like that at anything but a snake. Quick, Anand, quick!"

Anand was moving fast. He took the fork from Rama's hand. They all backed away as he lifted out a forkful of hay, dumped it on the ground, and lashed out at a tiny wriggling green-and-brown object.

Now all was still in the barn.

Anand spoke first. "A Russell's viper," he choked out. "One of the deadliest snakes in all India. Our little

Peppy would have been dead in five minutes. But how —how did this thing get into our barn? I filled the bins myself only while you were talking to those boys, Rajah. And the bins had just been washed out." The keeper was trembling now, fearing he was going to get the blame.

"It was that old juggler," Kamala cried. "I saw him from the wall top when I was trying to catch Moti. He was out behind the barn—just after Anand brought Peppy out for the class."

"But didn't I tell you, Kamala, that you were not to play around the barn here?" The Rajah was quite pale. He went over and took the rope from his daughter's hand. "Why...you might have been killed."

"Yes, but isn't it a good thing I did come here today? And what if Rama hadn't brought Moti along? And what if I hadn't chased her into the barn here where she screamed at the snake? And what if I hadn't been here to help Rama, holding the cow...." Kamala's voice was rising higher and higher. Suddenly she burst into tears.

The Rajah handed the cow over to Anand. He took her close in his arms. "All right, all right," he said soothingly. "But something terrible might have happened to you, little one." He looked back at Anand.

"Could it possibly have been that old juggler? Oh, no. It's just too ridiculous. A snake could have come in from anywhere."

Anand looked grim. "If you had heard him ranting last night under the banyan tree, Rajah, urging the villagers to destroy the cow—well—I know what *I* think."

The Rajah looked troubled.

"And what's happened here this morning is not going to make things any better. You know how the villagers look on the killing of a snake. A curse will fall on us. Any bad luck we have from now on will be because of this." He pointed down at the dead snake, then burst out, "No, we must keep this quiet. Not a word to anyone. *Anyone*, remember. Do you understand, boy?" He was looking at Rama.

Rama nodded mutely.

"And here, grass-boy," Anand shoved his six annas into his hand, "is the money for your straw. Take your monkey and go."

"Come, Moti," Rama choked out, and the monkey, looking very subdued now, came running down and leaped into his arms.

But at this point Kamala burst out, "Rama's a very brave boy. I think Anand should keep him and his monkey here in the stable, where they could tell us if any more snakes are around."

72

The Rajah smiled and patted her head. "You've still got your eye on that monkey, haven't you, mischief?" he said. But he turned to Rama then, and said seriously, "Yes, you were a very brave boy. And a bright one too. You should be in our new school." He pulled a rupee from his pocket and put it in Moti's little paw.

VII   The Blue Monkey

Outside the gate Rama paused to knot the six annas safely in his loincloth end. But the rupee he tucked in his turban. The baker's wife called to him as he hurried on. "Is my blanket nearly ready, Rama? I'm packing my daughter's wedding boxes today."

"It's going into the dye vat tonight," he assured her. "It will be ready tomorrow."

Any other time he would have gone on his way singing over the six annas tied in his cloth. He would have raced into the courtyard to tell the wonderful news about the rupee in his turban. But he remembered the Rajah's order; and if he told about the rupee he would have to tell of the snake, so kept silent. He was glad both the women were too busy to notice him. Grandmother was over at the vat, vigorously paddling air into the dye, making sure that the baker's blanket would have the rich blue shade which had given the weavers their fine name. His mother stood in the shade of the mango tree, taking her work from the frame.

"Did you get the six annas, son?" Grandmother called out. As the head of the family she handled the money, watching every pice, hoarding it in the tin box buried in the mud floor to buy rice for the next season's seeding. "Did he ask for more?"

"More what?" He had quite forgotten the straw.

"Well, never mind. We'll lose more than six annas if we don't get out soon and chase off those thieving paddy birds. Here," her voice was suddenly gentle and she shoved him a handful of peppery sweets, "get along, boy. But you..." she was cross again as Moti came skipping down from the wall, tiny paw outstretched. "Where have you been all day, you mischief? She broke loose right after you left this morning, Rama...."

"She..." he caught back the words just in time. After all, he could not tell about Moti without telling about the snake too. And that would bring loud wails from Grandmother, who never failed every morning to put her offering of rice or marigold before the door of the snake down in the mustard field, hoping to ward off evil.

He made his way down into the paddy field, climbed up on the bamboo stand, and began to shout and beat on an old can to scare off the birds. But they merely rose lazily in a cloud and settled back down again. And after a time his thoughts began to wander. He began to think of Dumbir. He had not driven his herd by again tonight. Had the villagers spoken the truth this morning when they said he was no longer going to be a herdboy, but a student—as a reward for bringing Peppy in? Rama's face clouded. If only he had driven her straight on into the village! If only the juggler had not been there spying with his evil eye! Still—he felt at the rupee still safely stowed away in his turban—if he had won the reward, how could he go to school and leave Grandmother and Mother to do all the work? Who would drive the oxcart? Who would get the indigo leaves? Who would scare off the paddy birds?

His brown face was broadening again into its usual cheerful smile. He laughed aloud as he suddenly remembered how the little flying cow had broken from the class that morning and run to him. She knows me, he told himself proudly. The old juggler had been wrong when he had said a curse would fall on anyone who touched her. She had brought him good luck already. He felt again at the rupee in his turban.

Then suddenly, remembering the snake, frowned.

And the first words he heard when he went home again at sundown were about the juggler.

The blanket was now off the loom, rolled up on a mat ready for the vat. Grandmother was still paddling air into the dye. The rice for the evening meal was already piled in a snowy mound on a plantain leaf on the mat which served as table. His mother was stirring something savory in the big black pot. They were talking of the news which the merchant had just brought in along with the ox and cart he had hired for the day. "*Ram-Ram-Ram*," Grandmother was bemoaning, "if some curse doesn't come on this village! Whoever heard of such thing before! They build a fine new house for a foreign cow and drive a poor old starving pilgrim from the bazaar."

"They didn't drive him from the bazaar, amma," Rama's mother, usually so meek, spoke with sudden spirit. "They just asked him not to sit near the barn and scare the new cow with his snake flute."

"Our Hindu cows have never minded the snake flute. . . ."

"But why does he play the flute when he has no snake? Just to get the villagers around so they will listen to his wild words. The merchant says he has started real riots in some villages."

Rama made haste to unyoke the ox and take it out to bathe it in the pool in the river bed. He gave its dusty rumps an extra dousing. He bathed himself and rinsed out his turban—making sure the rupee was still safe—and wound it wet around his head. Then he led the ox back home. All was at peace now. The moon was rolling up like a great golden ball behind the mango tree. His mother was dishing up a bowl of the savory vegetable curry. There was a feeling of great contentment as they ate their meal.

"We'll take the blanket out of the vat at dawn," Mother said, glancing with relief at the loom now stacked empty against the wall. "Then we'll stretch it in the sun. It will be dry by sundown. Then you will take it to the baker's wife and we'll get that ten rupees." She sighed happily, then looked around suspiciously. "Where is Moti tonight?" she asked. For Moti's absence usually foretold trouble.

"She was sleeping out in the paddy field under the stand when I left her," Rama said.

"Don't worry. She won't miss her rice." Grandmother's sharp old eyes had already spotted the plantain tucked in under her grandson's cloth. "Aha," as a shrill cry sounded out from the well, "and there she is." They all started up in alarm as a dark, twisted mass came hurtling over the wall, straight down into the vat, bringing a great hunk of clay with it.

There was a moment of silence; then Moti let out a feeble spluttering cry, and Rama raced to rescue her. He fished her out, dripping, caught fast in some dirty, muddy cord.

"Alas, alas, our fine dye!" the women began to wail.

"What is this?" Rama untangled his pet, and she, still gasping for breath, slunk away to hide her shame. He shook the net out—such a one as hunters used to snare birds in the jungle, and which now sent a shower of muddy dye over them all. His voice rose high in wrath. "Why, it's that old juggler's. I saw it in his basket last night. He's been trying to steal my monkey."

"You mean your monkey's been trying to steal his net." Grandmother was looking down at her stained sari. "A good thing we didn't put that blanket in the vat before supper."

"Yes but the baker's wife is waiting for it. And the moneylender is waiting for the ten rupees. I told him tomorrow." Mother drew her sari across her face, and Rama knew she was crying.

He stood miserable, not knowing what to do. He glanced anxiously toward the corner of the courtyard where he had just heard a feeble cough.

"Well," Grandmother spoke briskly. She patted Mother's bowed head. For all her sharp tongue she had a warm heart and much sense. "No use crying over muddy dye. The vat can be cleaned out. There's more water in the well. And there are more indigo leaves out on the plain. You, Rama, you will be off at dawn for another load. And that monkey of yours will be tied fast all day to make sure she gets into no more mischief."

Rama's heart swelled with happiness. He had fully expected that this time she would give that dreaded order—*get rid of Moti*.

He darted across, gathered up his monkey and took

her down to the pool in the river bed. "No, I know you don't like water," he scolded as he doused her up and down. "But just look at you." He made haste to dry her as she began to shiver and cough. He spoke more gently, "But why do you get me into so much trouble, little one? Some of these days the juggler really will get you—oho!" He burst out laughing. "If he should see you now he certainly will. He'll carry you off and show you at the fair—a blue monkey." Moti peered intently down at herself, at her coat no longer pale gray but bright blue and frizzy. She plucked out a hair and held it up questioningly; then, when Rama laughed again, she jumped down, overcome with shame, and ran off crying.

Rama went on back to the courtyard. He took up the net and went out to the well. And there, as he had expected, sat the old juggler again, eyes closed, basket beside him. Rama threw the net down before him. "Here you are, juggler," he said.

The juggler opened his eyes and spoke smoothly. "Ah, the weaver's son again. That monkey of yours is a real tricky one. I was sitting here tossing my net, making it disappear up into the air as I do in my shows, when, bless me, it actually did—up into the mango tree and over your wall."

Rama did not answer. He liked the old man even less when he had a smooth tongue. At that moment, though,

Moti began barking angrily from the branches above. She appeared out in the moonlight and hurled a little green mango.

The juggler made a strange, raspy sound meant to be a laugh. "Oho, weaver's boy, it's you who should be the juggler. You've changed your Moti into a blue monkey." His eyes took on a crafty look. "You know I could use such an animal in my shows. Here, boy, how much do you want for her?" He pulled out an old moneybag, suddenly eager.

Rama reached for Moti and held her close, shaking his head no.

"Come, boy, a rupee. Two rupees..." the voice was rising as it had the night before under the banyan tree. He scrambled to his feet, and Rama shrank back. The monkey was quivering close to Rama now as the juggler came closer, shaking his moneybag before his face. "What's the matter with you, weaver's boy, standing here like a starved crow, letting silver slip through your fingers! Don't you know what silver can do for you?"

Rama shrank back further, his arms tightening around his monkey.

"The Rajah called you a bright boy. You would rather have his silver words." The old man's voice rose in shrill imitation. " 'You're a bright boy—you should be in our new school,' he says. Bah!" He shook the bag under Rama's nose. "School would be wasted on a dolt like you. Your head, like your monkey's, is thick and meant only to carry a load of straw. I offer you two rupees—no, *three*—for that scraggy animal of yours, but you let it slip through your fingers just as you let those five rupees slip into the herdboy's hand—the rupees that should have been yours for finding the flying cow."

Rama's eyes were big with fear. *He knows everything*, he was telling himself.

"Yes, yes, yes," the juggler gave the cackly laugh again, "you lug the cow all the way in from the plain—then let the lazy herdboy lead it in through the Rajah's gate and claim the reward. A dolt you were born, a dolt you will die. But let me warn you, boy," his eyes were blazing fanatically again, and his bony fingers reached toward Moti, "I'll get that monkey."

And now Rama, made bold by fear, cried, "No, no,

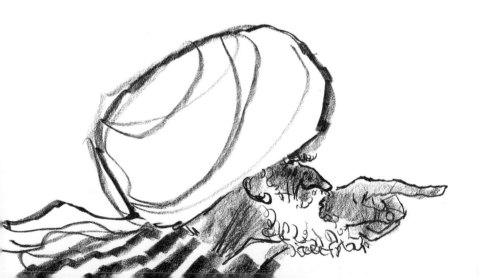

no, juggler. You want her only to kill her as you would have killed the flying cow this morning with your snake!" He gave a violent thrust that sent the old man reeling back over his basket, down into the dust.

Moti leaped screaming up into the tree.

Rama stood terrified at what he had done and said. But the juggler after a moment got to his feet. He shook out his turban and put it back on. He reached for the net, shook it out, rolled it neatly, stowed it in the basket, and put it on his head. Then he turned and shook his staff at Rama, "A curse be on you, weaver's boy!" he said.

Rama stood watching as the juggler disappeared off toward the plain. He was still trembling. Then suddenly he felt Grandmother's hand on his shoulder. "Better the curse than the gold of the evil man, son," she said quietly.

Rama did not know how much she had heard, and she asked no more questions. But, like the juggler, he told himself as he followed her back into the courtyard, Grandmother knew everything.

VIII   The Cheetah

Rama was off to the plain again at dawn. He would
come back early, he told himself, and take another load
of straw along for the flying cow. He made sure that
Moti was home, tied fast. He kept a wary eye for the old
juggler as they went creaking in through the cactus. Just
in case the old man was listening, he made up a song—
as Hindu boys all do—to let him know how he felt about
things. He sang at the top of his voice:

> *Rama, the brave one, now behold,*
> *I fear not the curse of the juggler old.*
> *I fear not the cheetah, nor the flying cow,*
> *When she flies by, salaam I cry.*

He broke off, grinning at the foolish mistake they had all made over the cow. Then he went on:

Deep in the jungle, friends I see,
In the Rajah's barn Peppy runs to me.
Soon I shall wear a coat of white,
And guard her safely all through the night.

His spirits rose with the sun. The old juggler's curse had not worked, he told himself as the day wore on. True he had had to go a long way to find the indigo again; but when he finally did they were fine big plants, and he filled the old cart in no time at all. He found rich grass, too, and a big load was swinging out behind as they started for the village. He had kept up his song all day. Tonight, he told himself, he would sing it to his mother and grandmother as they sat in the moonlight, and they would all laugh together. "*H-r-e-e-e,*" he shouted so gaily that the old ox caught his spirit and went trotting off at a speed that set bell jingling, cart creaking. On the way he passed Dumbir's water buffaloes wallowing in a pool, big noses just showing above the muddy water. He stopped singing and looked around for the herdboy.

He had not seen him since that last moment at the Rajah's gate. Dumbir was known as the teller of tales, a boaster of brave deeds; but he was not really bad. He shouted curses at Moti—but then Moti chased his herd.

85

It was shame, over claiming the reward unfairly, that was keeping him in hiding now, Rama knew. "Dumbir!" he shouted.

He shouted again and again. He glanced at the sun. It was a long way from the village, and the herdboy should be starting the buffaloes homeward by now. The ugly big beasts were already lumbering to their feet at the sound of his voice.

He climbed out and hunted around the pool, calling, "Dumbir, Dumbir," growing more worried as the moments passed with still no answer. He glanced back toward the teakwood forest, which herdboys always avoided. It lay silent all day but at dusk was filled with voices of many wild animals. It already looked dark and forbidding. But suddenly, as he stood straining eyes and ears, he thought he heard someone calling. He started running.

And as he came closer to the forest edge he was sure he heard "Rama, Rama, Rama..."

"Dumbir!" he shouted again. He shoved in through the dank undergrowth.

"Here, Rama—up here." Dumbir's voice came tremblingly from above him. Rama peered up and saw the herdboy's face peering down through the leaves, eyes rolling in terror.

"What's wrong?" Rama whispered, looking anxiously around him now.

"It's a cheetah." Dumbir's teeth were chattering so Rama could scarcely get the words. "I lost one of the buffaloes and came in after it, and here was a big cheetah...."

"A cheetah!" Now Rama was always singing about the cheetah. But the one he sang of was that tiny helpless baby he had found dying on the plain. Of all the wild animals which came out of the teakwood forest at night, the real cheetah was the most feared. It lurked in the long grass waiting to spring on the hapless cow or buffalo forgotten by the herdboy. It even raided the courtyards and pens in the village, carrying off goats and chickens and calves. "Where?" he choked out now.

"Right there, where you are."

"How long ago?"

"Just now. I fell and hurt my ankle, and when I got up there stood the cheetah just ready to spring on my buffalo. I yelled—and got up the tree here—and the buffalo ran..." Dumbir was openly blubbering now.

"You're sure it was a cheetah?" Rama looked around, grew braver when he saw nothing. "Did you really see it? Or just hear it?" Another of Dumbir's stories, he was beginning to tell himself.

"I saw it. I heard it. You know that funny barky noise they make—not a roar like the tiger, nor a scream like the elephant. You know, a noise like this—*bak-bak*..." Dumbir let out a very real cheetah bark.

"No, don't—don't! That will bring him back!" Rama was as frightened as Dumbir now.

"And I saw him," Dumbir insisted, "A huge big cheetah, bigger than I've ever seen before. With great black horns growing out of the side of his mouth...."

But now Rama burst out laughing. He knew it was just another of Dumbir's stories. A cheetah with horns. "Like your cow with silver wings, eh, Dumbir," he jeered.

"No, no." Dumbir was actually crying again. "I swear it was a cheetah, and it had horns. And he stood there lashing his tail...."

"All right, then we'll scare off the evil one with his horns." Rama turned, raised his voice high, "Come, cheetah, come, cheetah!"

"Rama!" Dumbir's agonized whisper silenced him. "Look—*there!*"

Rama turned. And there stood Dumbir's giant chee-tah, a great, sleek creature with golden black-spotted coat and long slender legs, small proud head with eyes glowing like jewels, tail uplifted, swaying gently back and forth, and—*yes, Dumbir had been right*—two narrow black horns curving upward from his mouth, giving him a most evil look.

He was standing in a small clearing, making a low purring sound. As he stepped forward his paws crackled the leaves beneath them. He let out a little bark.

But Rama too let out a cry—of joy. He went tumbling forward and put his arms about the cheetah's neck,

resting his face against the horned one. "Little brother, little brother," he was whispering almost tearfully.

The cheetah nuzzled his head against him, raised his paw, and playfully tapped him. His great purrs filled the woods now. He lay down and rolled over, coaxing for play. Rama ran his fingers down over the furry belly, ran his fingers too down over the horns—the ugly black scars which ran from the corners of the mouth to the edge of his eyes. He stood back to admire him when he rose again, then went up, took the head between his hands and murmured proudly, "Ah, you are indeed a rajah of the forest now." And the cheetah, understanding, gave an assenting purr.

But suddenly, at the sound of a wooden elephant bell, he was on the alert, tiny ears perked, tail poised rigid. Without warning, he turned and disappeared back into the bushes.

"Come, Dumbir," Rama cried, "the teakwood cutters are coming. They will take you into the village, and I'll drive your buffaloes."

Dumbir, wincing with pain, let himself down out of the tree. He had watched the scene between Rama and the cheetah in open-mouthed wonder. By the time he had hobbled out into the open, however, the sound of the wooden bells was dying in the distance.

Slowly, and with Dumbir groaning all the way, they

made their way back to the cart. Dumbir tumbled in on top of the indigo leaves and, with the buffaloes trailing along behind, they started on toward the village. After a time, Dumbir began to recover. He edged up close to Rama and began to tell of the terrible encounter he had just had. "You know, Rama," he said, "for a moment when I saw the big cheetah about to spring on my buffalo I was too scared to move. Then I grabbed my stick and ran toward it. And what an ugly brute it was with those great black horns...."

Rama burst out laughing. "This is the story you are getting ready to tell the villagers under the banyan tree tonight, eh, Dumbir? It isn't the one you told when you were hiding up in the tree."

Dumbir grinned foolishly, then said, "Yes, you really are very brave, Rama. I used to laugh when I heard you singing out on the plain about how you were not afraid of the cheetah, and how all the animals in the jungle were your friends; but now I know you spoke the truth. Tell me," he drew closer, spoke seriously, "what is this spell you put on the cheetah and the other wild things to make them roll on the ground and play with you when they attack everyone else?"

"I have no spell," Rama said.

"Oh, yes you have. Come. I won't tell, Rama. How is it you're not afraid?"

Rama laughed. "I sing because I *am* afraid. The song scares the cheetah away."

Dumbir shook his head.

"And, as to that cheetah today. There was nothing strange about that. He was my little baby one—you remember, the one I found out on the plain two years ago. Don't you remember him?"

"Oh, no, not that monster!"

"Yes, but he is. I knew him at once by those black scars on his face. You called them horns, but they were just the marks where he had cut himself on the thorns when he was lost on the plain. Don't you remember how my grandmother put herbs and ghee on to heal them? And today he was rolling on the ground just as he used to when he was a kitten." Rama laughed softly. "And he a rajah of the teakwood forest now."

"Oho—if I had known that." Dumbir spoke in a changed tone now. He sat up, looked out ahead, and saw that the top of the Rajah's palace was showing in the distance. He saw too that his buffaloes were straying behind. His ankle was suddenly better.He slipped out of the back of the cart and, letting out a whoop at his buffaloes, went after them.

IX   *The Plotters*

Rama was glad to be alone. He drove on. What a story he would have to tell to his mother and grandmother tonight! But thinking of them made him remember the wilting indigo leaves, and he tried to hurry the ox on.

It was slow going though now for his search for Dumbir had taken him off the road, far back into a tangled part of the plain. More than once they had to back out and find another way. And once, as they stopped in a particularly bad spot, the old ox looking reproachfully around at him, Rama thought he heard a voice.

He waited a moment, then, hearing it again, jumped

out and went to look. As he edged between the cactus he began to get words quite clearly and suddenly recognized the loud ranting voice. He had heard it often in the past few days. He edged on more warily, then abruptly almost tumbled out into a clearing.

The juggler was standing down in a little hollow making another of his wild speeches. Rama's eyes widened when he saw how many important villagers were in the crowd circled around him. There was Suberu, the Rajah's steward. And the goldsmith. And the moneylender—yes, and some of the guards who usually stood at the Rajah's gate.

The juggler was pounding his staff on the ground. His voice was not that of an old man at all. His words carried far back into the cactus where Rama stood listening. "If your village is not to be destroyed by our gods then you must atone and make sacrifices. You must destroy this evil foreign thing that has come into your land. I ask you, villagers, are you going to send your sons to this school to drink in these vile teachings—that all men are equal; that the Creator meant the Rajah to live with the outcaste, the outcaste marry the merchant's daughter. . . ."

"No, no, no," the crowd broke out angrily.

"This new school is a breeding place of poison," the juggler went on, "where your sons will learn to despise our sacred Hindu books, our temples—where the foreign cow will be set up as king and our sacred Hindu bulls and cows penned up behind gates...." His voice was rising higher, and with it the anger of the crowd.

Rama himself was growing so excited he almost forgot himself, and again came near to tumbling out into the open. But at that moment the steward broke in with a loud, "All right, juggler. But why all the talk? What are we to do about it? The cow stands in the new barn. The school is already crowded with the sons of Brahmins and outcastes. Give us the answer. Or have you one?"

The juggler pounded his staff again. "The same answer I have been giving all up and down this sacred land of ours. The answer I give to all these young upstarts who go off to foreign schools and come back filled with foreign poison for our sons to eat."

"What is the plan, juggler?" It was the moneylender speaking now. He owned most of the cows which roamed the lanes.

"Yes, what is the plan? We're ready, whatever it is," the crowd echoed. They were working themselves up into a frenzy now.

The juggler made a sign for silence. They crowded close as he went on, slowly, clearly now. "There is only one way. The Rajah has started out to destroy all the

Creator gave us—the plant life, the ants, the cobras. He
sprays his poison powders over all the land. He brings
in these vile foreign cows to breed with our sacred
Hindu ones, so that our children will drink vile
foreign milk."

"Cut out the words, juggler," someone shouted,
"what are we to do?"

97

"You must destroy the foreign cow. Destroy the foreign school. Destroy the books that are putting poison in your sons' minds. Here is my plan." He motioned them all to draw closer. He spoke in tone lowered, but still clear enough to reach Rama's ears, "Tonight the Rajah will be out of the village. The school will be closed. The guards can be overpowered. By the time the Rajah returns his precious school and cow will be ashes—sacred ashes which we will offer to our gods to atone."

The crowd broke into a shout. But Rama did not wait to hear more. He fled back to his cart, let out a loud *h-r-e-e-e,* and hurried on his way.

X   The Riot

It was dark by the time he drove through the river bed
into the village. Leaving the ox to make its own way
home he raced on to the palace. Tonight was full moon,
and many of the villagers had gone with the Rajah to
the next village to the festival celebrating Ganesh, the
elephant-headed god of the crops. The lanes were deserted. So too was the bazaar when he came to it. Nor
was there a guard at the palace gate or a watchman at
the school. He went timidly on down past the big
white buildings, now silent and dark for the weekend.
He began to run when he spotted a light in the barn
behind. The main building was all in darkness; but the
door was open, and he could hear the cows in their
stalls and see them outlined against the walls. Then
someone moved in the room beyond.

"Anand!" Rama cried out.

"Is that you, watchman?" Anand's voice answered.
"No. It's Rama, the weaver's son." He ran across and
stood in the doorway of the experimental room.

"Ah, the grass boy who found the snake, Rama."
Anand had turned, smiling; but now, seeing Rama's
face, he got to his feet. "What is it, boy?"

"They are going to kill the flying cow tonight. They
are going to burn down the barn." Rama began. "I
heard the old juggler out on the plain, and he..." His
words were tumbling out in a jumble now.

Anand drew him in and closed the door. He glanced
toward the iron-barred window. "What is this?" he
demanded. "Say it slowly. You mean that juggler is still
making trouble?"

Rama spilled out the story again. Anand listened,
growing more grave each moment. He looked around
the room, then went out and peered into the dark barn.
"I should have known something was wrong," he said,
talking more to himself than to Rama now, "no watchman on duty, half the guards gone from the palace."
As though just taking in what he had heard, he broke
out in great agitation, "But we must do something about
this, quickly. You go, boy...." He stopped. "No, no...
they wouldn't let you in, wouldn't listen to you. I'll
have to go myself. I'll go to the palace and get them to
send a fast messenger after the Rajah. You will have to

stay and look after things here." He closed and bolted the big barn door and glanced toward the back ones already shut for the night. "Keep everything barred till I come back, Rama, understand? Don't let anyone in. I'll be back in just a minute." So saying he ran back into the other room, put out the light, and left by another door.

Rama stood looking about him. The moon was now up, and the bars on the window were casting long thin shadows over the white floor and the stalls of the happily munching cows. He edged in beside Peppy and put his arm about her satiny neck, whispering, "No, no, Peppy, they must not hurt you. That evil juggler must not get you." And Peppy, as though understanding, put out her rough tongue and licked his arm, nuzzling for more caresses.

Rama stood waiting for Anand's footsteps. He grew more anxious as the minutes dragged on and there was still no sound but the munching in the stalls beside him. But finally he did catch a faint one, coming in from the back and from the distance.

Ram-ram-ram, he prayed. He ran to the end of the barn and peered out, straining to catch the sound. It was rapidly growing louder. It's just the villagers coming back from the festival, he told himself, and they have been drinking too much palm wine.

But the sound was louder now, and he knew it was
not from merrymakers but from angry rioters. Once
before when he had been a little boy he had heard such
a noise. It had been that year of the great drought, when
there had not been enough rice to eat and the people
had stormed the merchant's stall. Grandmother had
taken him up close in her arms and fled with him out
to the plains. Yes, he had heard it before, the same kind
of growl the tiger in the jungle made just before he
sprang. He shrank back when torches began to flicker
along the fenced-in pasture. And now he could hear

things cracking and crashing, and tiny flames were licking along the ground.

He looked frantically back into the barn. "They are coming this way, Peppy," he cried out, "and they are going to burn down this place. What shall I do? Anand! Anand!" His voice rose shrill.

But by now flames were rising from the big straw stack not a stone's throw from the window. They were racing ahead of the rioters, even driving them back. Clouds of smoke were billowing through the barn. The cows were going wild. Rama's eyes were streaming. But now he told himself he could no longer wait for Anand. So, flinging wide the big doors, he raced back to unloose the five village cows first, leading them out one by one, turning them into the garden. By the time he got to Peppy flames were leaping up just outside the window.

"Come, Peppy," he coaxed; but the little flying cow, dazed and blinded, stood firm. Rama tore off his turban, plunged it into one of the buckets of water which stood at each stall, and slapped it over her face. "Come, Peppy," he said again firmly, and she followed him into

the open. Flames were crackling now on the barn roof. Rama and the cow went dashing through the crotons out to the street.

By this time a crowd had gathered, some moaning, some praying, some blaming the rioters, others the flying cow. But all were sure the fire would eat up not only the Rajah's fine palace, but their own palm-thatched homes.

No one noticed the weaver's son tugging a cow out through the smoke. No one saw him start hurrying it down one of the narrow dark lanes.

"Come on, Peppy, we can't stay here," he cried, when she began to pull back. A sniff of smoke started her on. By this time heavily laden oxcarts and villagers with great bundles on their heads and babies in their arms were heading for the plain. They kept to the main road, however, and when Rama turned down his own lane he found it deserted. Deserted too was his own courtyard when he finally tugged Peppy in.

"Amma! Amma!" he cried anxiously. He bolted the gate and looked around him. The indigo plants lay in a heap on the ground. The muddy dye still filled the vat as it had that morning. But the brass water jars, the cooking pots, the oxcart—and Grandmother and Mother —all were gone. "Amma!" he shouted again, but his only answer was a sad little whimper from the cow shed.

He dropped Peppy's rope and ran across to free the monkey, who had been in jail all day for her part in the previous night's disaster. She came out, still in her blue coat, looking very ashamed. She leaped up into his arms and, crying, buried her face in his neck.

Rama turned and looked back at the sky. A red glow still hung over the bazaar. And there was a steady stream of villagers passing the well outside. "We can't stay here, Peppy," Rama whispered. But Peppy, who had already found the waterpot, was now munching on marigolds. She rolled her big eyes around as though to say, what's wrong with this?

Rama stood frowning, then suddenly burst out, "We will go to the old Buddha temple!" It lay not too far off and in a tangle of cactus that kept everyone from it. Generations before, the villagers had stopped offering rice and flowers to the huge smiling figure which now lay toppled in the dust. The little shrine on which the idol had once rested was still standing, but was said to be haunted by evil spirits. "But they can't be worse than that old juggler," Rama muttered.

"Yes," he went on to Peppy, who had rolled her eyes again at the sound of his voice, "that is just where we will go. But, alas, how am I to get you there? The plain is full of spying eyes tonight. If only you had those wings Dumbir gave you, then you could just fly off!

Or if only you had great wide horns, and a hump on your back, and a long white face! If only," he patted her satiny flank, "you were not so clean and shiny, but..." his face brightened, "we can fix that!" He grabbed up a bit of rag, sopped it in the dye vat and ran it down over the pale gold body. It left a dirty streak which, Rama knew, would, in just a few moments, in the air, turn bright blue. He glanced up at Moti, perched on the wall now, very interested in what was going on. A funny little bright blue monkey. Rama shook his head. "No, no, Moti, we can't have her looking like you," he said. "A blue monkey and a blue cow ...we must find something else." He looked frantically around; then, spurred on by fresh sounds in the distance, his mind and fingers began to work fast. He seized up some of the clay Moti had knocked from the wall two nights before and dropped it into the dye. The next moment he was giving Peppy a coat of the dirty mixture. He smeared the velvety black face with whiting which Grandmother used to paint scrolls on the courtyard floor, then bound a great load of straw on her back to hide the telltale lack of hump. He tore off the fine red halter and twisted a bit of old rope about her neck. Then he stood back to study the result. "Alas, poor ugly little one," he whispered ruefully.

For, indeed, Peppy, the proud little foreigner, in her

dirty coat, looked exactly like all the other millions of cows that roamed India's lanes. She did not seem to mind, though. She stood chewing the roll of marigold, regarding him serenely through her new long white lashes.

Rama took a last quick glance around the courtyard. He took time out to place a marigold before the household god in the niche up in the wall, breathing a prayer that Mother and Grandmother might be safe. Then, with waterpot on head, Moti on shoulder, he grabbed up Peppy's rope and started off.

They went down through the mustard field, keeping to the deserted part of the village. Rama tightened his hold when they crossed the river bed and Peppy sniffed down toward the reeds. They made a queer-looking group as they zigzagged across the plain, in and out around the cactus clumps, the tall brown boy with the blue monkey perched on his shoulder and the heavily laden spotted cow. But at last they came to the hiding place.

There was nothing much left of the temple now but the four walls of the shrine on which the big Buddha had once sat. Moonlight flooded the pile of refuse, dead leaves and vine-clad broken pillars. But Moti's joy at finding a resting place told there was no snake lurking; and the flying cow, once inside and tied fast to a pillar, lay down and slept. The monkey edged in beside her and slept too.

Rama piled stones high across the narrow entrance and for a time kept watch across the plain. But the red glare had died down over the village. The top of the Rajah's palace gleamed white against the deep-blue night sky. The voices were no longer those of angry men but of the wind rustling in the reeds, the jackals crying in the distance.

Rama sank down, too, and slept.

XI Dumbir Sees a Ghost

Rama had gone to sleep with his mind full of riots and burning barns and evil jugglers, so it was little wonder he started up in terror when he heard someone crying for help just after dawn. He looked dazedly around the strange place he was in, at the cow with its load of straw all askew on her back, nibbling happily on green vine. Then as the cry came again from outside, his senses came to him. He scrambled up on the top of the barrier he had made and peered out.

He had recognized Dumbir's voice, and there, wavering like black shadows in the low-lying morning mist, were Dumbir's buffaloes milling around. And there was

Dumbir himself—only the upper half of him showing—
eyes rolling in terror at the little blue monkey who,
perched on top of the old idol, was about to hurl a
second stone.

"Drop it, Moti, drop it!" Rama ordered. He jumped down and hurried out to Dumbir, who, however, as he neared him, turned and fled down the road screaming in terror.

"Wait, Dumbir, wait!" Rama raced after him and overtook him. He seized the end of his cloth and held him fast. "Whatever's the matter with you? It's Rama, your friend. What's happened in the village? Is the riot over?"

But the herdboy's eyes were rolling terror. He pulled away, choking out, "No, no, no. It can't be. You're dead, Rama. You were burned in the fire."

At another time Rama would have laughed; but after the terrible night, and seeing how Dumbir was actually quaking, he said soothingly, "Don't be so silly, Dumbir. Look at me. Here I am. I got out of the fire and came out here to hide. And that was Moti—just teasing you," he ended lamely.

"That? Moti?" Dumbir glanced up at the little blue creature perched on the Buddha's head and let out another wild, "Oh, no, no, no," and disappeared into the mist.

Rama stood frowning. The mist was now clearing and the village in the distance was emerging, looking just as it always did. What had happened there? If only Dumbir had not been so foolish, taking him to be a ghost, he could have found out whether the riot was over—and if his mother and grandmother were safe. Oh, why had Dumbir been so silly! Well, Rama told himself grimly, I'm just going to stay here till someone comes along who will tell me the truth.

The morning dragged by slowly, though. The sun rose high. Peppy had long since finished the water in the pot and was bawling loudly for more. Rama was too scared to venture even to a small pool which he knew lay nearby. Moti, still sulking over her scolding about Dumbir, had climbed back up on the Buddha's head and now sat staring sadly out over the plain. Suddenly she let out an excited *beep-beep* and came skipping down. Rama caught the sound of elephant bells.

He sprang to his feet and saw the big royal elephant padding swiftly toward the shrine. And riding up in the howdah on top was the Rajah himself with his little daughter Kamala, and Anand the keeper, and—Rama fairly rubbed his eyes, for such a sight he had never thought to see—two village women in white widows' saris, *Grandmother and Mother*. There was actually a lump in his throat as he went scrambling down to meet them.

The elephant knelt to let them all dismount. Rama cried out, "She's safe! She's safe! Peppy's safe!" Then

before they could stop him he went clambering up to
bring her out.

"See!" he cried happily.

But the little group stood dazed, staring at the queer-
spotted animal with its long white eyelashes, and the
load hanging crazily now to one side.

"But that's not our flying cow," the Rajah began.

"Oh, yes, yes, it is, O Rajah. I changed her to look
like a village cow. See!" Rama tugged the load off. "I
didn't want them to see she had no hump."

The Rajah burst out laughing. The others joined in. Mother and Grandmother ran forward to embrace Rama. Now they all were crying and laughing and talking at the same time. But finally the Rajah managed to make himself heard. "We had just gone to your house this morning," he said, "to tell your family we feared you had perished in the fire which destroyed, happily, only part of our new barn last night. But just as we..."

"We had just come in from the plain where we had been hiding all night in the oxcart," Grandmother broke in excitedly, quite forgetting she was interrupting the Rajah, "and your mother had just picked up a fine red halter over by the dye vat. 'What is this?' she said, but just at that moment..."

"...and then just as the Rajah was telling us you were dead," Mother broke in, voice all trembly, "in rushes that nitwit Dumbir, shouting that he had seen your ghost out at the shrine here. And he said an evil blue spirit had chased him and hit him on the head with a stone...."

"But as soon as we heard those words, *evil and blue,* we knew it could be none other than that wretched Moti," Grandmother took up the tale again. "And if Moti was alive, then Rama might be too, we said, our dear brave Rama." Her voice broke.

"Brave Rama indeed!" The Rajah echoed with feeling, "That is what all the village is crying today. They say you saved their school, perhaps the whole village. They are seeking some way to reward you...."

"Reward me?" Rama looked troubled. He patted the cow, who, in turn, reached out her rough tongue, to touch his hand, "I was only trying to save Peppy. You see she sort of belongs to me. I've been getting her out of trouble ever since that first day she fell out of the sky into the Black Oil Pool. The day the juggler told me he was going to kill her—and that I would end up dead, like the black crow."

The Rajah cast a startled glance toward Anand, but he spoke quietly to Rama. "But why would he say that, weaver's son?"

"Because I told him I was saving all my money to go to school some day."

"You mean you want to go to school?" the Rajah broke in.

"But I didn't have enough money yet—and someone must help Mother and Grandmother...."

"But if that is what you want you shall be in school tomorrow morning." The Rajah's eyes shone with pleasure at Rama's wish.

"I start to school tomorrow morning," Rama said with disbelief.

"Yes, but come, everyone. We have much to talk

about, much to clear up, but just now we must get this poor tired boy, and this poor tired cow, back to the village." The Rajah climbed back up into the howdah, followed by Kamala with Moti in her arms, then Mother and Grandmother. "You ride with us, Rama, Anand can bring in the cow."

Rama cast a troubled look around the plain. "But the juggler?" he demanded.

"We have the juggler tied up fast in jail this morning," the Rajah assured him.

"But remember, he's a juggler," Rama said.

The Rajah smiled. "I don't think he'll be able to undo the ropes we've got around him this time. Come, boy, let us go."

But Rama still hung back. He looked around at Peppy who, as Anand went to take her, lowered her head in a most threatening manner. "I think," Rama said boldly, "You had better all go on ahead and let me bring in Peppy by myself. She has had a bad scare, and is not sure about the elephant. She ought to be with someone who knows her and how to handle her."

The Rajah smiled at Anand. "He's right," he said. "We don't need to worry about either of them. Rama is coming to our new school to learn many things about cows; but there are many things he is going to teach us. I see a new master for our school some day not too far off."

Indian Words and Names

ALWAR (*all*-war). A boy's name.

AMMA (*um*-maw). Mother. Also used to address any woman, as "Ma'am."

ANAND (a-*nund*). A boy's name.

BABU (baw-*boo*). A gentleman or student, used as "Sir."

BANYAN TREE. One of the largest and longest-lived trees in the world. Village council meetings are held between its hanging roots, and temples are built alongside it.

BUDDHA (*bood*-da, the *oo* as in "foot"). A young king, born in 560 B.C., who gave up his throne to become a holy man helping the poor and needy. He taught that happiness in this life and the next could come only by forgetting self and showing love and pity to all living creatures. He founded one of the great religions of the world. Giant figures of Buddha and thousands of jeweled shrines to him can be found all through the East.

DUMBIR (dum-*beer*). A boy's name.

DURGA (*door*-ga, the *oo* as in "poor"). A goddess who controls disasters. Gifts are given on her festival day, which corresponds to Mother's Day.

FAKIR (faw-*keer*). Properly used, a holy man who can perform miracles; commonly used to refer to tricksters and beggars.

GANDHI CAP (*gun*-dee). The small white cap worn by admirers of India's great leader, Gandhi.

GANESH (*gun*-ish). The elephant-headed god who guards the crops and flocks of the villagers and wards off bad luck.

GHEE (*gee*, with g as in "get"). Melted butter.

HINDU. One who belongs to the Hindu faith. The majority of Indians are Hindus, believing in many gods to whom they offer gifts either in fear or worship. They believe that the soul of man passes at death into the body of another human being or animal and for that reason will not kill, nor eat flesh. They believe mankind was created in four *castes*, or classes, and man must stay in the class into which he was born. Religion enters into every act of the Hindu's daily life.

HOWDAH (*how*-da). A seat placed on an elephant's back to serve as a seat for four or more persons.

INDIAN MONEY. 4 pice (rhymes with "ice") equals 1 anna. 16 annas equal 1 rupee (roo-*pee*). A rupee is about 20 American cents.

KAMALA (*come*-u-la). A girl's name.

MAHOUT (*mah*-hoot). An elephant driver or trainer.

MANGO TREE. A beautiful blossoming tree which bears large, luscious, red-gold fruit. A sacred tree mentioned often in Hindu books.

RAJAH (*rah*-ja). A prince.

RAMA (*rah*-mah). A Hindu diety; used as a boy's name. *Ram-Ram-Ram* is a contraction of Rama, used so commonly as an exclamation of wonder, grief or anger that it has become slang.

RANI (*rah*-nee). A princess.

SALAAM (sah-*lam*). A greeting, either by word or by touching palm to forehead. Varies in different parts of India.

Sari *(sah*-ree). The seven- to nine-yard length of fine gauzy material (coarse homespun for a widow) draped artistically to form a dress for the Hindu woman. The style of wearing varies in different parts of India.

Ser or seer (pronounced *seer*). A two-pound measure, sometimes more, sometimes less.

Tulasi plant *(tool*-a-see). The sacred shrub found in every Hindu's garden, around which he chants his prayers. Leaves are given for good luck as wedding gifts and to cure sickness.

Turban. A five- to seven-yard length of muslin which the Hindu winds around his head as a hat or, as in the case of coolies, as a pad for loads. There are many ways and skills in turban winding, each district and caste having its own.

Wick. The small earthen saucer of oil in which a bit of wick is lighted, giving the only light most villagers have.